P9-ARZ-655

Charlie
and the
Blanket Toss

TRICIA "NUYAQIK" BROWN • ILLUSTRATED BY SARAH "ANUYAQ" MARTINSEN

ALASKA
NORTHWEST
BOOKS®

"Yay-hey-hey!!"

Charlie heard his father's happy shout. He knew what it meant:
a whale had given itself to the people!

Today the whaling crew's flag would fly over the captain's house—
our house! Charlie thought—as a sign to the whole village. *Good news!
Our crew was successful!*

Every family in the village would enjoy some fresh boiled whale meat
and **maktak**•, the skin and blubber.

•*MUCK-tuck*

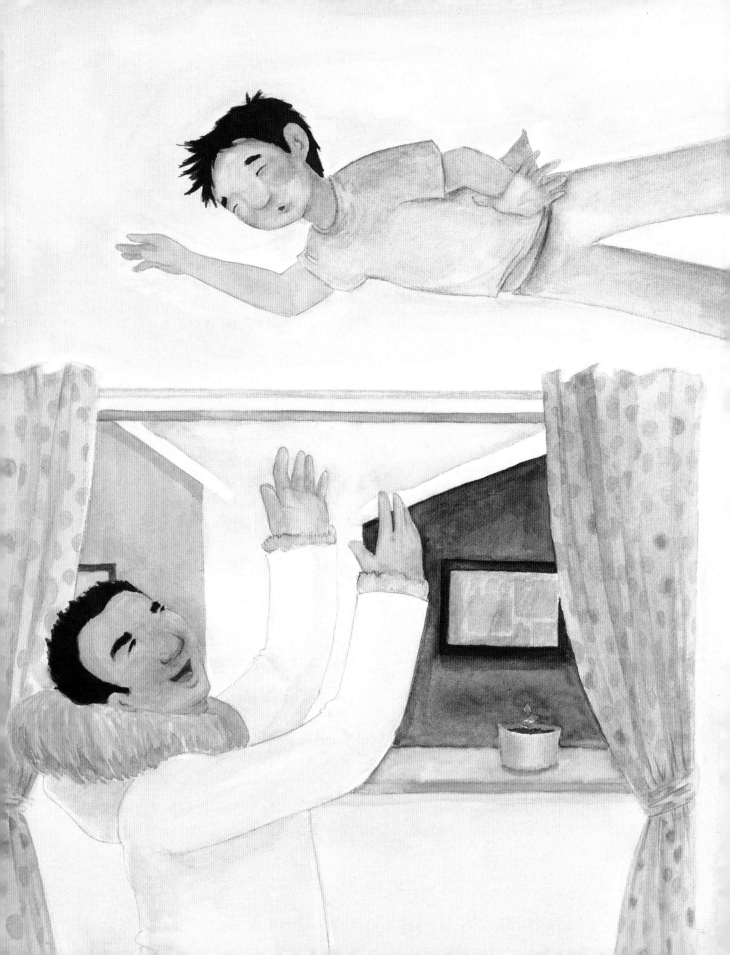

C̲harlie hopped in place and clapped as Dad pulled Mom into the folds of his hunting parka. Then Charlie threw himself in to join the hug. Suddenly, he was shouting, too, as his father tossed him up-up-up!

"Whoaaaaaaaa!"

At the very top, where up meets down, Charlie shut his eyes and held his breath. His stomach did a flip. And then he was in his father's arms again, laughing and squirming.

"Just getting you ready for **Nalukataq***, son!" his father's big voice boomed.

*NULL-uh-kuh-tuq

*N*alukataq! The Summer Whaling Festival was Charlie's favorite *Iñupiaq*° holiday. Tradition said that those who caught a whale—his father's crew!—decided when the outdoor celebration would be, usually in June.

There would be an all-day feast, storytelling, drumming, singing, and dancing to honor the whalers who helped provide for the community. *And best of all*, Charlie thought, *the blanket toss.*

After dinner, grandmother shared a story about Nalukataq, telling it as she had heard it from her grandfather, and his grandfather before him, keeping memory alive.

"*Iñupiat*° people, for thousands of years, we take care of each other," his *Aana*° said. "One boat catches a whale . . . nobody starves. Pretty good reason for Nalukataq, eh?"

°*eh-NU-pea-ak*   °*eh-NU-pea-at*   °*AH-nuh*

nd did they always do the blanket toss, too?" Charlie asked.

"That is what **nalukataq** means—it is our Iñupiaq word about the blanket toss. We have no trees, so whale spotters climb the high ice ridges to look for spouting whales. And the blanket toss, well. . . . " Aana chuckled. "They say when my grandfather was a boy he could fly higher and see farther on the blanket than any of the men spotting from the pressure ridges. He wasn't much older than you."

"Do you think he was ever afraid, Aana?" Charlie asked quietly.

She waited a long moment before answering.

"Maybe, Charlie," she said. "But do not worry. When it is your turn, you will be ready."

That night as Charlie nestled into his pillow, he thought about the captains and their wives—the first to take turns on the blanket—throwing out candy while they were high above the crowd. Then he pictured his brother Bill's first time on the blanket.

Friends and family held the rope handles. Together in a steady rhythm, the circle of people slowly let the sealskin blanket droop, then lift, droop, then lift, and then . . .

POP!!!

They snapped the blanket up and tight. Bill flew up-up-up toward the Midnight Sun, his arms out and feet churning like he was riding a bicycle. When Bill came down, he landed as gracefully as a bird.

"Maybe this year, that will be me," Charlie whispered before he fell asleep.

As the weeks passed, everyone was busy getting ready. Charlie's Uncle Robert helped fasten new rope handles onto the **mapkuq**, the tough sealskin blanket.

*MUP-kook, *CA-me-piak, *AH-tee-ghee

His mom sewed new sealskin **kamipiak°**, traditional boots, for Bill and Charlie, while Aana worked on a pretty spring **atigi°**.

And cousin Paul and the other crew made sure the whale meat and maktak were ready for serving.

The whole village seemed to be looking forward and waiting.

inally one June morning, Charlie opened his eyes and the big
day had arrived.

Nalukataq!

Outside, the sun lit a cloudless blue sky, so bright that Charlie had to
squint. Slabs of shore ice were still piled up in places, but the deep cold that
pinched his nose and made his eyes water was gone.

Strong sheets of plastic made a windbreak so people could
sit comfortably, talking, eating, and keeping warm.
Charlie raced ahead.

Boom . . . Boom . . . Boom . . .

Charlie followed the sound of the drums. His aunties, girl cousins, and his friends' mothers were practicing in a neat row, dressed in pretty *atikłuk*• and cotton gloves. Late tonight they would be performing to honor the whalers.

Although their feet didn't move, their heads and arms told the song's story. Feet together, knees bobbing with the beat of the drums, the gentle grace of their arms . . . Charlie loved it all.

•*AH-tik-look*

Then the song was over and his Iñupiaq teacher, Ms. Piquk, was leaning toward him.

"Charlie, how old are you now? Old enough for the blanket toss, I bet."

He started to answer, but another song suddenly filled up space between them, and he didn't have to finish.

Y um! Charlie followed the scent of **uqsrukuaqtaq°**, homemade
donuts, that hung in the air. Steam drifted off giant, simmering
pots of fresh game and whale meat. Long tables held caribou soup, duck
soup, goose soup, **mikigaq°**, stewed fruit, cakes, cookies, tea, coffee, and
hot chocolate. *And akutuq°!* thought Charlie. *The world's best ice cream!*

The hungry boy ate until he was full, but there was still a little room.
He was holding out his bowl for more caribou soup when he noticed
Auntie Katherine was serving him.

"Is that you, Charlie?" she cried. "Look how big you've grown! Big
enough to go on the blanket this year, eh?"

"Um. . . ." Charlie's words wouldn't come, and fear tickled his very
full stomach. "Maybe. . . ."

But Auntie didn't hear him. She was already ladling soup into another
bowl, so Charlie slipped away.

°ook-shrewk-coo-ak-tug   °MICK-kee-gak   °ah-GOO-tuk

C harlie, there you are!" Dad threw his arm around Charlie's shoulder. "Come on, son. We need strong young men to help the servers."

Dad and his crew had filled cardboard boxes with generous cuts of meat and maktak. It was time to evenly share the bounty of the hunt, as their ancestors had done for generations.

"*Quyanaq*• . . . thank you," Charlie heard friends and neighbors say over and over as his heavy box grew lighter. "God bless you."

He was so proud of his father, so proud to be walking among the men of the whaling families, he thought his heart would burst. Someday, he hoped, Dad might be just as proud of him.

Maybe today? Charlie wondered.

•*KOO-yah-nak*

That afternoon, Charlie and his friends left the grown-ups for some
    kid time. They chased balls, played tag, and explored the shore.
    Through it all, he pretended not to think about his big decision.
Is anybody else scared about flying higher than the roof, or is it just me?
    Just then he heard a roaring cheer:

"Aarigaa•! Whooaaaa! Ui, Ui, Ui•!"

With a start, Charlie realized the blanket toss had begun. *How did I miss it?!*

Charlie sprinted toward the sound, his friends trailing behind him. With each quick step, he worried, *Will I be too late?*

•*AWE-rea-gaa* •*OO-ee*

Out of breath, Charlie got there just in time to see Bill fall from the sky and land gently at the center of the skin. Bill slid off the blanket, right in front of Charlie. He grinned, his cheeks red from the wind and the workout.

"Come on, little brother. Now's your chance. Are you ready?"

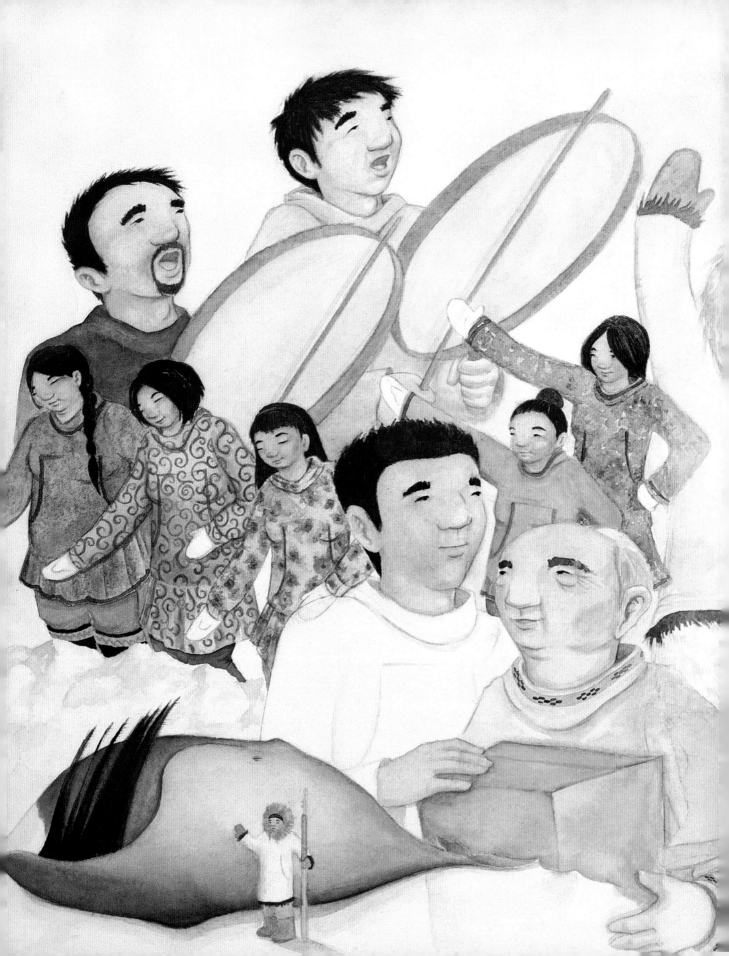

Hardly a moment passed before Charlie answered, but in that moment, many images flashed through his mind: a whale lying on the shore ice, a gift to his people. Dancers happily moving to the thunder of drums and Iñupiaq songs. The servers sharing the maktak and akutuq with the proud elders. And something he had never seen, but could only imagine: a long-ago boy who flew the highest and saw the farthest.

"I am ready," Charlie said.

The Iñupiat Whaling Tradition

The people of Alaska's arctic coast—the Iñupiat—cannot remember a time when they didn't rely on the migrating bowhead whales to help feed them. Eating whale meat and *maktak* is not just a menu choice, it is a vital part of being Iñupiaq, a sustaining tradition that has been unbroken for thousands of years.

Catching a whale has always been a very spiritual event, bathed in thanks and prayer. There is much gratitude toward the animal itself, which has sacrificed its own life to sustain the people. In the days of Charlie's great-great-grandfather, the Iñupiat hunted from open, canoe-like boats, which they made by constructing a driftwood frame and sewing bearded sealskins to stretch over it. While some traditionalists still make *umiapiaq*, or skin boats, modern hunters more often use metal skiffs and power motors during whaling season, so speed makes up for stealth. But it is still very hard to catch a whale.

To make sure the whales are not overhunted, the Eskimo Whaling Commission assigns each Iñupiat community along the coastal villages a maximum number that they may harvest per year. As a result of respectful regulation, bowhead whale numbers are increasing, and the people are still nourished by this important traditional Alaska Native food.

Barrow villagers celebrated Nalukataq under the flag of a successful whaling crew in this photo that's more than a century old. (Alaska State Library, Rev. Samuel Spriggs Photograph Collection, P320-36)

Iñupiaq Eskimo Words

Aarigaa! (AWE-rea-gaa) "Good job!"

Aana (AH-nuh) grandmother, great aunt

Akutuq (ah-GOO-tuk) traditional ice cream made from whipped *tuttu* (caribou) fat, mixed with ground and shredded *tuttu* meat

Atigi (AH-tee-ghee) pullover parka

Atikluk (AH-tik-look) summer dress cover

Iñupiaq (eh-NU-pea-ak) a "real" or "genuine" person; also, the language spoken by the Iñupiat people

Iñupiat (eh-NU-pea-at) the Eskimo people of Alaska's far north

Kamipiak (*CA-me-piak*) traditional boots with soles of hard, crimped bearded seal-skin or soft winter *tuttu* (caribou) skin. Uppers are made from caribou hide, seal-skin, wolf, and/or calfskin.

Maktak (MUCK-tuck) blubber and skin of a bowhead whale, eaten raw or frozen

Mapkuq (MUP-kook) traditional blanket made from the whaling captain's boat cover. Each corner of the square is strung to a post that keeps it lifted.

Nalukataq: the Summer Whaling Festival; also word for tossing people on the mapkuq

Na – the "a" is pronounced like the short u sound

lu – the "u" is pronounced like the double oo of "cook"

ka - the "a" is pronounced like the short u sound

taq – the "a" is a short u sound; the "q" is a uvular sound made in the back of the throat

Mikigaq (MICK-kee-gak) fermented whale meat with blubber and tongue

Quyanaq (KOO-yah-nak) thank you

Ui! (OO-ee) an outburst by men who are dancing, tossed in the air, or just wholeheartedly happy

Umiapiaq (Uh-mia-pea-ak) traditional boat with a wooden frame covered with bearded sealskin

Uqsrukuaqtaq (ook-shrewk-coo-ak-tug) dough fried in oil

Conrad Stinson, this one's for you.
—T. B.

*For my nurturing parents, Dorothy and Andy, my loving husband,
Matt, and the warmhearted people of the North Slope, who have
shared their home and its wealth of inspiration with me.*
—S. M.

Quyanaq to Fannie Akpik, Katherine Ahgeak, and other Iñupiaq friends, who
have generously shared their cultural knowledge and experience for this book.
We are very grateful to Ruth Outwater Cox, Alice Nashookpuk,
and Jack Oktollik for the gifts of our Iñupiat names.

Text © 2014 by Tricia Brown
Illustrations © 2014 by Sarah Martinsen

All rights reserved. No part of this book may be reproduced
or transmitted in any form or by any means, electronic or
mechanical, including photocopying, recording, or by any
information storage and retrieval system, without written
permission of the publisher.

Library of Congress Cataloguing-in-Publication Data
Brown, Tricia.
    Charlie and the blanket toss / by Tricia Nuyaqik Brown ; illus-
trated by Sarah Martinsen.
        pages cm
    Summary: Charlie, an Inupiat boy, is excited about the upcom-
ing festival to celebrate a successful whale hunt, but afraid when
he thinks this might be the year he takes part in the traditional
blanket toss. Includes glossary and notes on Inupiat whaling
traditions.
    ISBN 978-1-941821-07-7 (hardcover : alk. paper) 1. Inu-
piat—Juvenile fiction. [1. Inupiat—Fiction. 2. Self-confidence—
Fiction. 3. Festivals—Fiction. 4. Alaska—Fiction.] I. Martinsen,
Sarah, illustrator. II. Title.
    PZ7.B8185Ch 2014
    [E]—dc23
                2014012775

Editor: Michelle McCann
Designer: Vicki Knapton

Published by
Alaska Northwest Books®
An imprint of

GRAPHIC ARTS
BOOKS®

P.O. Box 56118
Portland, Oregon 97238-6118
503-254-5591

www.graphicartsbooks.com

Printed in China